ATTICUS BLACKWOOD

CONTENTS

CHAPTER 1

LONG DRIVE THROUGH WASHINGTON

Washington undergoes a wondrous transformation into a captivating winter wonderland that never fails to impress. As I gaze outside, I'm treated to the breathtaking sight of snow gently cascading down the mountain slopes, creating a mesmerizing scene that never loses its charm. The fluffy snowflakes delicately settle on the pine trees, painting a beautiful picture of gray-white against the deep green needles. Amidst the pristine snow-covered landscape, I discover a few Jasmine and Pansies flowers peeking through, their vibrant hues standing out against the snowy backdrop. However, this magical setting was overshadowed by a rather unpleasant hunting trip experience that left a sour taste in my mouth.

My Dad and his friends would embark on an annual deer hunting excursion to Washington. This year, I was fortunate enough to join my Dad, as it was winter break. My mom wasn't thrilled about the idea of bringing an 8th grader on a hunting trip, but my

Dad insisted, believing it would toughen me up. The journey to Washington was lengthy, and I recall spending hours gazing out the window, yearning to have my Nintendo Switch with me. Regrettably, my Dad strictly prohibited any video games for the entire trip.

During the journey, I found myself frequently catching a glimpse of my reflection in the truck's mirror. I would often stare at the image, trying to discern the sadness in my expression. All I could make out was the striking contrast of my bright, curly red hair against my tan-white skin. The freckles scattered across my nose couldn't escape my attention, and I couldn't help but notice how dissimilar I looked compared to my father. Despite both of us having the same hair, skin, and freckles, his massive red beard matched his formidable lumberjack physique perfectly. He exuded a ruggedness that made it seem like he could effortlessly hurl a log over a mountain. In contrast, my slender, frail frame would struggle to lift even a twig. Nevertheless, I cherished the opportunity to spend quality time with my father.

As the car rumbled down the road, I hesitantly voiced my thoughts, "I appreciate the time we're spending together, Dad, but why did it have to be a hunting trip?" My father's eyes remained focused on the road ahead, but his unmistakable grin conveyed his response, "Well, Joey, I thought you might enjoy getting out of the house and embarking on an adventure with me. You're always holed up in your room playing video games, so I felt it would be nice for us to get some fresh air."

I could see where my Dad was coming from, but I couldn't shake off my hesitancy. "I get your point, but why hunting?" I voiced my concerns. "I don't feel comfortable with the idea of taking an animal's life, especially when I find peace and fresh air at school," I explained. My Dad's smile dimmed slightly. "It's not the same. Hunting will teach you real-world skills that you can apply in your daily life. Like the art of patience. Learning to wait for the right moment." I glanced out the window and let out a quiet sigh. "I understand that, but I learned patience from playing video games. You need a lot of patience to outmaneuver your opponents," I tried to reason. My Dad sighed in return, "Son, why are you okay with shooting in video games but not with providing dinner?" he asked. I shrugged, "Well, for starters, it's not real, and no one gets hurt. So, why bother catching dinner when I can just order takeout?" My Dad looked frustrated and rubbed his forehead, "Son, you can't always rely on others to bring you food, and why are you so fixated on these games?" I turned my gaze to the window, hoping to divert the conversation. "Because I want to become a successful YouTuber, live-streaming myself playing games and making a fortune," I revealed. My Dad's lack of enthusiasm was hard to miss. "Is that really what you want? To stay indoors and play video games all day and miss out on real-world experiences?" I crossed my arms and looked away, feeling a sense of disconnect. "I knew you wouldn't understand."

As we made our way towards the cabin, the atmosphere inside the car was heavy with silence, and I couldn't shake the feeling that my Dad was lost in his thoughts. The winter landscape outside was a breathtaking sight, with snow covering everything as far as the eye could see. However, my attention was soon captured by the sight of the grand hunting cabin looming in the distance. The cabin stood tall and imposing, a two-story structure crafted entirely from the finest redwood, giving it a regal and timeless quality as if it had been carved from the heart of a majestic maple tree.

The exterior of the cabin was adorned with intricate carvings, each detail adding to its undeniable charm. The roof, slanted and snow-covered, added to the picturesque scene. Wisps of smoke lazily drifted from the chimney, dissolving into the crisp winter air, accompanied by the comforting sound of crackling wood. The front yard was a vast expanse of pure, untouched snow, transforming the entire area into a winter wonderland. Wooden rocking chairs and a fire pit took pride of place on the inviting front porch, beckoning us to come and make ourselves at home.

While the front of the cabin exuded warmth and comfort, the side revealed a large pool cloaked in a pristine blanket of snow alongside a hot tub that seemed to promise soothing relaxation. The steam rising from the hot tub created a mesmerizing dance with the cold air, and I could almost feel the comforting warmth against my skin from afar. Through the cabin's windows, a warm orange glow emanated, giving the impression of a crackling fire casting its cozy light within. Faint sounds of laughter and chatter added to the welcoming ambiance that enveloped the cabin.

As my Dad parked the truck and hurriedly retrieved our bags, the sounds of clinking glasses and hearty laughter floated through the air, indicating the safe arrival of Dad's companions. Despite the stunning appearance of the cabin and the warm reception, a sense of unease lingered within me, hinting that this trip might not unfold entirely as anticipated.

CHAPTER 2

A GOAT STARES ME DOWN

Upon entering the cabin, my gaze was immediately captured by the stunning exterior. However, it was when we crossed the threshold that I was truly struck by the breathtaking interior. The soaring walls were adorned with an impressive display of animal heads, including majestic deer, formidable bears, wild boars, and magnificent elk. The sheer quantity of trophies was awe-inspiring, indicating the owner's deep passion for hunting and an impressive collection of hunting triumphs.

The grand stone fireplace, reminiscent of a castle, dominated the space, its protective steel gate shielding us from the crackling embers. Despite the barrier, the fireplace exuded a welcoming warmth, instantly enveloping us. In front of the hearth lay a vast bear rug, its jet-black fur so deep that it initially appeared as a void in the floor. The fixed gaze of the bear's head lent it an uncanny lifelike quality, sending an involuntary shiver down my spine.

The cabin's furniture exuded luxury, with its supple leather and inviting comfort. Several recliner chairs and a spacious U-shaped couch were placed perfectly in front of the crackling fireplace, creating an ideal setting for engaging conversations. The rest of the house embodied the ultimate mancave, featuring a ping-pong table, a poker table, a pool table, and a grand bar. The bar itself complemented the interior with a massive wooden table, six barstools, and an impressive assortment of spirits.

Adjacent to the bar, a staircase led to the second story, where we discovered a captivating wrap-around balcony that seemed to lead to our rooms. However, nothing quite captured our attention, like the striking gun wall. Adorned with an array of bolt-action rifles, shot-guns, semi-automatic rifles, and a couple of crossbows, the sheer quantity of weapons showcased the serious dedication of the cabin's owner to the art of firearms.

As I ascended the stairs, the distant sound of laughter floated from the kitchen below. My dad had advised me to settle into my room while he caught up with his friends. Opting for the room at the far end of the balcony, I pushed open the door and was immediately captivated by its beauty. The gleaming polished hardwood floors reflected the soft light, and I caught a glimpse of my own reflection as I stepped inside. The wooden bed, dresser, and nightstands imbued the room with a cozy and rustic ambiance. The bed, a sprawling king-size, looked irresistibly comfortable.

A large window overlooked the forest, offering a mesmerizing view of the snow-covered trees. It was like peering into a stunning painting. As I gazed at the scenery, I suddenly sensed an eerie presence. Whirling around, I found nothing but the tranquil sight of the trees outside. Determined to dismiss the feeling, I began unpacking my bag, only to be seized by the sensation once more, this time more intense. I cautiously approached the window, straining to discern any sign of another presence beyond the glass.

I fixed my gaze on the location where I sensed a pair of eyes watching me, and suddenly, a shiver ran down my spine. There was a vague figure, but I couldn't discern its form. However, two yellow orbs were visible, locked onto mine. I strained to see more clearly, and then I realized that the pupils were slanted and doubled, resembling those of a goat. I pondered whether there were goats in Washington, given its mountainous terrain. I continued to stare, attempting to comprehend what lay before me, when something uncanny occurred.

The indistinct form began to move, and I witnessed its rise, not in the manner of a goat, standing on its hind legs, but like a human. It was a horrifying spectacle, causing my heart to race. I was overwhelmed by an unexplainable sense of dread and knew that I had to depart. Taking the lamp from the desk, I sprinted towards the door. In my haste, I thought I saw the goat-like being taking a step toward me, and that's when I realized that I had to escape as swiftly as possible.

CHAPTER 3
MEET MY DAD'S FRIENDS

As I left the room, clutching a lamp, I accidentally collided with what I initially mistook for a wall. As I stumbled and fell, I gazed upward to behold a towering figure - a man standing at an impressive height of 6 feet 9 inches. His countenance was adorned with a wide, welcoming smile. He was attired in a striking ensemble - a verdant flannel shirt paired with slate-colored pants. A voluminous beard of a dusky hue shrouded his entire visage, leaving only his eyes and nose visible. Crowning his head was a charcoal-hued skull cap, from which cascaded a mane of raven-black hair.

In a genial manner, the man addressed me, exclaiming, "Well, if it isn't Joey! It's been ages, my boy. How have you been, and why do you find yourself carrying a lamp?" He seemed perplexed by my sudden appearance with the lamp. As I righted myself, I gingerly placed the lamp on a nearby table. "Hey Ethan, it's been quite some time. Oh, the lamp. I was simply attempting to relocate it to a more suitable spot." I chose not to divulge the fact that I had been startled and hastily fled the room. "Hey Ethan, by the way, are there any goats outside?" I inquired. In response, he quipped, "There certainly should be. Goats are a delightful culinary choice. I concoct a marvelous stew using goat meat."

As Ethan and I made our way down the creaky wooden stairs, the air grew warmer, and the cozy aroma of the kitchen welcomed us. The room was alive with the sound of my dad's friends chatting and laughing, their casual sips of beer punctuating the air. At the head of the table sat my father, his familiar presence anchoring the room. Next to him was Ben, the youngest member of the group. Despite his youth, Ben possessed the lean, agile frame of a seasoned hunter. He sat with an aura of quiet confidence, his eyes betraying a keen awareness of his surroundings.

On Ben's left sat Alex, a man of seasoned strength and quiet charisma. His smooth, bald head and impeccably maintained grey goatee exuded an air of wisdom and resilience. His solid build hinted at a lifetime of weathering both physical and metaphorical storms. Directly across from Alex was Daniel, a rugged figure cloaked in a camouflage jacket. His strong, muscular frame and shadowy stubble hinted at a life lived amidst the untamed wilds, a hunter and explorer at heart. Beside Daniel, Oliver held court, a robust Texan with a neatly trimmed beard and a weathered cowboy hat. His imposing presence and warm smile added a touch of Southern charm to the gathering.

"Hello, everyone," Ethan's booming voice echoed through the room. "Say hi to Joey. He has a question for every-one." As I stood among the tower-ing figures, everyone rose, greeted me warmly, and gave me encouraging pats on the back. I felt diminutive in the presence of these six-foot-tall giants. "So, what's the question?" Ben in-quired. "Well, there was a goat out-side my window, and I thought I saw it stand up like a man." Anticipating ridicule, I braced myself, but to my sur-prise, there was none. Oliver turned to my Dad with a spark of excitement and declared, "See, I told you those myths were true, Noah." My Dad looked contemplative as he glanced down and absently stroked his beard. "I guess this trip will be exciting after all," he mused. "Hey, Joey, is there anything else you can tell us?" Alex inquired. Feeling perplexed, I asked, "Wait, what's going on? What myth are you all talking about?" I turned to Ethan, who raised his hand and added, "Yeah, I would like to know what's happening too."

Ben presented an old newspaper article with a grainy image of a goat-like creature standing on two legs. I couldn't believe it - that was exactly what I had seen outside my window.

"So, wait, is this thing real?" Alex questioned. "Well, Oliver seems to think so, and he's proposing that we go hunting for it," he added. With a wide grin on his face, it was clear that Oliver was eager to embark on this adventure. "But if this creature is real, shouldn't we consider its right to exist?" I interjected. Oliver chuckled and replied, "That's exactly why we need to act quickly before authorities get involved. Come on, Noah, we need to do this. It could be the greatest hunt in history." As my dad settled into his chair, he remarked, "It would be quite the thrill to pursue a creature that most people believe to be mythical, like hunting for Bigfoot." Ethan jokingly defended Bigfoot's existence, and everyone burst into laughter. "I think we should track down this goat-like creature," Daniel asserted. "Agreed, let's capture ourselves a goat, man," Alex chimed in. "We're in, except for Ethan and Noah. What do you say?" Ethan confirmed his participation, and after some consideration, my dad also joined in. With their beers raised, the group let out a cheer.

I expressed my concern to the group, "Wait, are you all sure about this? What if the goat man is endangered? What if it's the last of its kind? We don't have the right to kill it!" In response, Oliver shot me a disapproving look. "Noah, what have you been teaching this boy?" my Dad interjected, followed by a nonchalant shrug. "He's not really into hunting, but I thought this trip would change his mind and get him out of the house more." I gazed at my Dad, silently questioning whether he was truly okay with what was happening. Then, Oliver directed his attention to me and delivered his perspective, "Look, boy, you can't stop the thrill of the hunt. Yes, we hunt for food, but we also hunt for the love of the game. The game also puts food on your table. You should appreciate your Dad for bringing you along so you can learn how to survive in nature. Our ancestors were hunters and took pride in it, and you're standing over here worrying about if this creature is the last of its kind. I'll tell you this: nature is not friendly. If that goat man had a choice to eat you, it would. So, it's better to get it first than get you." As he spoke, I observed everyone else nodding in agreement with what he was saying.

"That is nonsense. You just want to hunt and kill it to feed your ego," I said. Oliver did not like that and stepped up to me, but my Dad got between us. "Now look, give my boy a chance to change his mind. He'll probably have a different outlook once we get started," my Dad said. "I don't know, Noah. Your boy might be more of a gatherer than a hunter. Maybe he should look for some berries for us," Daniel said as everyone laughed. I didn't think this was right, but clearly, I was outnumbered. "Okay, Joey, stay at the house while we go into town to get more supplies. Don't leave or touch any of the guns on the wall," my Dad said. I told him I would stay put. They all grabbed their coats and walked out the front door. I heard two trucks start up and then drive down the driveway. I sat in one of the recliners, looking at the fire, thinking this would be the worst trip ever. Then I heard a loud knock on the door and the sound of keys turning the lock.

CHAPTER 4

I TAKE A FORGOTTEN PATH

I rose from my seat and hastily grasped the nearest object at hand, which turned out to be a striking statue of an owl. With the others having already departed, I couldn't help but wonder who might be waiting at the door. As I cautiously swung it open, I was met with a sudden jolt of surprise, causing me to blurt out, "Who are you?" The man standing before me swiftly

raised his hands in a placating manner and identified himself as Lucas, the
proprietor of the cabin. He inquired
about my identity while I fumbled and
accidentally dropped the owl statue. I
proceeded to offer my apologies and explained that my father and friends had
rented the cabin for the weekend. To
confirm his claim, Lucas presented his
ID, followed by the Airbnb account to
establish his ownership of the cabin. I
felt a pang of embarrassment, realizing
that this was the second time today that
I had been startled and almost fled in
fear.

As I gazed up at Lucas, who seemed to
be in his late forties, I couldn't help but
be struck by his imposing height, rem-

iniscent of my father's stature. However, his slender build was more akin to mine. His short, disheveled blond hair and neatly groomed beard contributed to a rugged appearance, while his sun-kissed complexion hinted at extensive time spent outdoors. His attire, evocative of a rancher, exuded a practical yet fashionable charm, suggesting a readiness for any escapade, perhaps even mountain climbing. I found myself intrigued by his dark brown accessory, which bore a resemblance to some form of animal hide, but I chose not to inquire further, not wishing to come across as impolite.

"Of course, this is your cabin, isn't it? Do you also engage in hunting?" Lucas strolled over to the bar and casually poured himself a drink. "Indeed, this cabin has been in my family for generations. Although I reside on the other side of town, I rent out this place during hunting season to earn some extra money. I primarily hunt to provide sustenance for my family and friends," he explained. Seating himself at the bar, Lucas took a sip of his drink. "My father's companions claim they hunt for sport. I've never quite comprehended that, but they argue that it's a tradition passed down from our ancestors," I remarked. Lucas gazed at me and responded, "That's one approach to hunting. Many individuals hunt for the thrill of the chase, but others, like myself, do it out of necessity. It's not a recreational pursuit for me when I need to put food on the table. I don't pass judgment because everyone is entitled to their own viewpoint, but I personally don't favor that style of hunting. Nevertheless, it's inconsequential. As long as hunters are willing to pay my rate for the cabin, they are free to hunt as they please."

As I surveyed my surroundings, I couldn't help but feel that the cabin didn't quite align with Lucas's survivalist philosophy. "If your focus is on hunting for sustenance, why have a cabin that seems more geared towards indulgence and luxury?" I questioned. Lucas chuckled heartily in response. "I designed this cabin to cater to those seeking a lavish experience because that's what brings in the income. If you were to see my personal living quarters, you'd find nothing but firearms and archery equipment. I don't require all of this extravagance to meet my needs." It was evident that Lucas was a shrewd and pragmatic entrepreneur.

"What do you mean hunting for survival? Couldn't you just go into town and order food or something?" I asked. Lucas put down his drink and walked over to the fireplace. "I meant what I said: I don't hunt for sport. I could easily walk to town and order a steak, but I respect nature and what it provides.

The meat I get from something I hunted for in the woods better benefits me and my family. That steak I would have gotten from town was probably raised on a farm, with all types of chemicals to make it grow faster. But the animals in the wild are grown naturally, with no chemicals, just nutrients from their surroundings. It's also rewarding knowing that what I eat is something that I put the hard work into catching. My wife is great at growing vegetables, so we always have something grown from the earth. Can you see what I mean now when I say I hunt for survival?"

I gazed into the crackling fireplace, finally grasping his perspective. "No one has ever articulated it that way before. I always assumed people hunted for the thrill of having a trophy on display." Our eyes wandered to the mounted animal heads on the wall. Lucas rested his hand on my shoulder. "As I mentioned, people hunt for various reasons. Oh, look at the time. I need to head out. I was planning to drop off some paperwork for your Dad, but I can catch up with him later. Where are they, by the way?" Peering out the window, I explained to Lucas my Dad's intention to pursue the elusive goat man. A concerned expression washed over Lucas's face. "I hope they locate this goat man. But you don't seem enthusiastic about it. Don't you desire a trophy from the goat manhunt?" I met Lucas's gaze and replied, "I'm apprehensive that they will find and harm it. I'm not fond of hunting animals for sport; my Dad expects me to partake. I simply aspire to be a YouTuber and indulge in video games. I value nature enough to admire its splendor, but I don't want to take its life for entertainment."

Lucas knelt down, his eyes meeting mine with a sense of understanding. "Joey, there's nothing wrong with feeling the way you do. I can see that you have a deep respect for the wilderness, more than you realize. Not everyone has to be a hunter, but we should all honor the spirit of our surroundings," he said. Standing up, Lucas walked over to the door. "Hey, Joey, if you want to truly experience the beauty of nature, take a walk on the trail behind the cabin," he suggested. Glancing out the back window, I spotted an opening in the woods that I hadn't noticed before. "What makes that trail so special?" I inquired. Lucas grinned and replied, "It's a magical path, in my opinion. If you have a genuine love for nature, the trail will lead you to something extraordinary. However, the path can also sense your true feelings, and if it senses that you don't appreciate nature, it will just guide you on a regular walk through the woods." I looked at Lucas and then back at the woods. "Is that really true, or are you just teasing me because I'm a kid?" I asked as Lucas wore a mischievous smile. "Why don't you go and see for yourself? The trail is known as the 'Forgotten Path.' Let me know what you discover, kid," Lucas said before leaving the cabin and closing the door behind him.

I found myself standing in the spacious living room, deep in thought about Lucas's words. Despite my father's strict instructions to stay indoors, I found myself unable to resist the allure of a walk along the trail. Hastily, I donned my warm coat and sturdy boots and cautiously slipped out through the backdoor. Each step through the snow felt heavy as I made my way toward the trail, determined to return before my father and his companions came back. Upon entering the woods, I gazed down the path and observed how the trees formed a natural tunnel, their branches intertwining above the trail. Steeling myself, I drew in a deep breath, summoned my resolve, and cautiously set foot onto the trail.

As I strolled along the trail, I was captivated by the enchanting splendor that enveloped me. The trees were blanketed in snow, and the pine needles glistened like frozen crystals in the crisp air. Fragrant jasmine flowers and vibrant pansies adorned the ground, casting a kaleidoscope of colors and fragrances that ignited all my senses like a symphony.

I was entranced by the sight of various animals frolicking in the snow as I ventured forward. Squirrels darted up and down the trees in playful pursuit while rabbits gracefully hopped along the path, their delicate movements leaving soft imprints in the snow. Even the raccoons observed me from their lofty perches in the trees. The rhythmic tapping of a woodpecker resonated from a distant tree, adding to the symphony of nature's beauty that surrounded me.

As I continued on my path, I was greeted by the sight of magnificent animals. Deer gracefully dashed past me, showing no fear or concern for my presence. Among them, a majestic elk strolled through the woods alongside the trail, its massive antlers towering above me. As I glanced back up at the treetops, I noticed the watchful gaze of owls, as if they were patiently observing my every move.

Suddenly, my steps came to a halt as I caught sight of a colossal black bear seated with its back against a tree. At first, it seemed as though the bear was asleep, and I contemplated quietly passing by. However, as I approached, I realized the bear was wide awake and gazing directly at me. In that intense moment of eye contact, fear gripped me as I comprehended that fleeing from this powerful creature was not an option.

As I continued along the trail, an unexpected encounter took place. To my surprise, the bear lifted its paw and gestured for me to proceed up the path. I was taken aback but cautiously walked past the bear. I could feel its gaze on me as I moved ahead, and as I glanced back, I heard the sound of its loud snoring. With a sense of bewilderment, I quickened my pace, periodically looking over my shoulder to ensure that the bear was not pursuing me. Although it remained stationary, I struggled to comprehend the unusual encounter.

Pressing on, I noticed that the temperature was rising inexplicably. The heat became so intense that I had to remove my coat. Despite the uncomfortable warmth, I persisted along the trail, and before long, the sound of crashing water reached my ears. As I approached the end of the trail, I was greeted by a breathtaking sight.

Emerging from the trail, I was greeted by the sight of a colossal waterfall nestled within a lush rainforest. The radiant sun illuminated the surroundings, bringing the vibrant flora and fauna to life. The once snow-covered ground had transformed into a carpet of verdant grass, extending from the forest to the base of the waterfall. Various creatures frolicked and played amidst the blossoming flowers, creating a scene of unparalleled beauty and serenity.

At the edge of the bubbling spring, there rested a weathered stone table upon which lay an enigmatic collection of items. As I approached, I discerned that they were reed pipes crafted from rich red oak and glistening in the sunlight. As I lifted the reed pipes, a gentle breeze enveloped me, imbuing the moment with a profound sense of connection to the untamed forces of nature.

Suddenly, a voice called out, "Well, hello, Joey, you finally made it." Startled, I turned to find a figure standing before me. He stood at my height with a sinewy, well-defined physique. His upper body was unclothed, revealing a sculpted chest and strong arms. Cascading down his back was a mane of flowing white hair entwined with an equally lengthy beard. His face bore a striking resemblance to that of a goat, with a pronounced jawline and sharp cheekbones. Two imposing ram horns emerged from his forehead, adding to his imposing presence.

Perhaps the most astonishing aspect of his appearance was his lower half, which resembled that of a goat, complete with lustrous white fur and powerful, muscular legs ending in formidable hooves. Yet, it was his eyes that captured my attention the most – the same luminous yellow goat eyes I had encountered earlier in the morning. "Who or what are you?" I inquired. With a genial smile, he replied, "Oh, pardon my lack of manners. Hello, Joey. It's a pleasure to make your acquaintance. My name is Pan, the God of the Wild."

CHAPTER 5

I MEET AN OLD GOAT..KINDA

Today has been quite eventful. It began with me reluctantly joining a hunting trip, where my Dad's friends ended up teasing me. After that, I encountered a cabin owner who directed me into the woods. And now, I'm in a surreal situation, standing before a creature who identifies as the God of the wild—an encounter so strange that I can't help but wonder if I've sustained a head injury during my trek through the woods.

"I couldn't believe my eyes. Was this place real? Was he real? I felt like I must be dreaming. After the terrifying encounter with those bears in the woods, I was convinced that I had met my end. But then, Pan started laughing heartily, clutching his belly. "Ah, you've met Bob! He's the guardian of my sanctuary and the reason you made it here safely." I was dumbfounded. "Wait, you're telling me that the bear I saw sleeping against the tree is the reason I made it here safely?" As I pondered all the animals I had encountered on my journey, Pan turned his gaze toward the forest, took a deep breath, and said, "My dear friend, nature is not always benevolent. It can be wondrous and generous, but it can also be harsh and unforgiving. Most of the creatures you passed by would have attacked or even attempted to devour you if Bob hadn't shielded you." I glanced back at the forest, recalling the creatures I had encountered. "But none of the animals I encountered seemed threatening, and none appeared likely to attack me, except for Bob, the bear." Pan kept his eyes fixed on the woods. "Bob was shielding you from the creatures you couldn't see." It dawned on me that I had felt a constant sense of being watched, even though I couldn't discern who or what was observing me.

I mentally made a note to express my gratitude to Bob when I departed.

I shifted my focus back to Pan. "Wait, are you saying that you're Pan, the God of the wild? Let's say I believe you. Why have you brought me here?" I couldn't help but wonder if I was still dreaming. Pan gazed into my eyes with his distinct goat-like features. "I brought you here so that you may champion my cause," he explained. I took a cautious step back. "Your cause? What do you mean?" Pan gestured towards the table and offered me a seat. As I sat down, he waved his hand, and an assortment of fruits materialized on the stone table, along with wooden cups filled with apple juice. If I wasn't dreaming, I found myself face to face with a deity who wanted me to support his cause, which I still didn't understand. The food looked delectable, and my hunger pangs were undeniable. I reached for a large, ripe apple and took a bite. Its sweetness was unparalleled. I couldn't resist and proceeded to devour the other fruits displayed on the table – each one more exquisite and exotic than the last: grapes, oranges, mangos, and pears. I glanced at Pan and observed him contentedly chewing on a tin can, just like a goat.

"Hey, Pan, what can I help you with?" I asked. Pan set down his tin can and replied, "You don't have to call me Mr. Pan; just Pan would do. I brought you here because I need people who are one with nature to take up my cause of the wild."

I was taken aback to hear that a deity needed my assistance and inquired, "How can I be of help? I struggle with math, let alone matters of such magnitude." Pan chuckled and explained, "It may seem peculiar, but it is crucial. As a god of the natural world, I rely on the aid of humankind to bring about my intentions. I preside over the untamed wilderness and the intricately balanced ecosystem. Unfortunately, humans have demonstrated a diminishing reverence for nature over the years. They construct chemical plants and haphazardly clear forests, spark mass deforestation, thoughtlessly dispose of waste into water bodies, and hunt defenseless animals. The world is slipping out of my grasp, and I urgently need individuals to protect what I cannot."

As Pan spoke, his wise and ancient voice echoed through the forest. "Throughout the centuries," he said, "we deities have learned that interfering too much with mortals can create chaos and disrupt the natural order of things. That's why we choose champions to carry out our will and protect what we can't." I could sense the weight of his words and the responsibility he was offering me.

"My powers were once much greater," Pan continued, "but gradually diminished over time as humans destroyed much of what I held dear. That's why I have settled here in Washington, where nature remains undisturbe,d and wildlife thrives in its natural habitat. The lush vegetation and free growth of plants make this place a haven for all who appreciate the beauty of nature. Even the humans here have come to appreciate and respect the environment around them."

As Pan paused, I felt the gravity of his request. "Will you take on my cause to protect the wild and everything it holds?" he asked. I put down my food and pondered his words. "But again, Pan, what can I do?" I asked. "I'm just a kid. What good could I be to you? Also, who else has taken on this cause? I can't be the first person you asked?"

Pan, with a serene expression, casually took another bite out of his tin can and began to enlighten me, "You are not the first. Many have taken up my cause, including John Muir, known as the father of the national parks, Theodore Roosevelt, a prominent conservationist and former President, Rachel Carson, a pioneering marine biologist and conservationist, Aldo Leopold, a renowned ecologist, and Wangari Maathai, an environmentalist political activist from Kenya." Intrigued, I asked Pan to elaborate on these remarkable individuals. Pan nodded and continued, "John Muir, a Scottish-American naturalist, founded the Sierra Club and played a pivotal role in establishing Yosemite National Park. Theodore Roosevelt, a conservationist, established five national parks and created the United States Forest Service. Rachel Carson, a marine biologist, wrote 'Silent Spring,' a groundbreaking book that sparked the modern environmental movement. Aldo Leopold, an ecologist and author of 'A Sand County Almanac,' championed a land ethic that encompassed all living things. Lastly, Wangari Maathai, an environmental and political activist, founded the Green Belt Movement in Kenya, focusing on environmental conservation and sustainable development."

I couldn't comprehend why Lucas had directed me to Pan, of all people. I was not an environmentalist; I simply admired the beauty of nature. "Why would Lucas send me to you?" I inquired. "I mean, I value nature and all that it provides, but I am not like those remarkable individuals who have contributed so much to its preservation. I fail to see how I could be of any assistance to you."

Pan approached me, his hand gently resting on my back, radiating a comforting warmth. "You don't have to conform to anyone else," he reassured me. "Your unique way of safeguarding nature is significant." He continued, "Lucas sent you to me because I understand your connection with nature. It's evident in your eyes and your very essence. You have great potential and could become an invaluable ally in our mission."

His words resonated deeply within me. I had never seen myself as someone capable of making an impact, but perhaps I could contribute in my own way. "So, you're asking me to join your cause?" I inquired. Pan nodded. "Yes, Joey. Will you embrace this challenge and stand with us to protect nature?"

As I stood on the edge of the clearing, ready to respond to Pan's question, a sense of urgency gripped me as I noticed the sky growing ominously dark. Realizing how late it had become, panic surged through me at the thought of facing my father's anger. "Pan, I need to get home right away. Can you show me the quickest route back to my cabin?" I implored, my voice betraying my anxiety. Pan seemed surprised by my sudden urgency but gestured towards the familiar path I had taken earlier. "We can go that way, but you must understand that without Bob's protection, you'll be vulnerable to the dangers I warned you about," he cautioned. Despite his warning, my fear of my father's wrath outweighed my fear of the wild. "I understand, Pan. I must leave now. Can I return tomorrow to give you my answer?" I asked, hoping to appease both Pan and my own conscience. Pan's smile was reassuring as he replied, "Of course, my boy. Just be cautious. The night is when the most perilous creatures emerge. I'll be waiting for your answer." With a nod of determination, I promised to return the following day and then turned swiftly towards the opening, sprinting with all my might in a desperate race against time to reach my cabin before my father.

CHAPTER 6

THE OTHER SIDE OF NATURE

As I sprinted through the thick forest, a creeping sense of doubt filled my mind. Was it a mistake to be here at this hour? The setting sun cast an eerie orange glow across the sky, transforming the once lively woods into a foreboding and unfamiliar place. The friendly, welcoming trees now appeared twisted and menacing, their gnarled branches reaching out like sinister claws. Every rustle of leaves and snap of twigs beneath my feet seemed magnified as if the entire forest was closing in on me. Despite the growing unease, I pushed myself to keep running towards the safety of the cabin. The encroaching darkness became my constant companion, its presence surrounding me like a malevolent force waiting to engulf me. Pan was right - at night, the wilderness became an entirely different realm, and I longed for the safety and comfort of the cabin.

As I dashed through the dense woods, desperate to find my way out, my thoughts kept circling back to Pan's earlier words. He spoke fervently about his mission to safeguard the wilderness and his quest to connect with kindred spirits. I couldn't shake off the feeling that his message didn't quite resonate with me. After all, I was just a young person, and my outdoor adventures were limited. My leisure hours were mostly spent playing video games and watching YouTube from the comfort of my room.

Despite my attempts to brush off Pan's rhetoric, it clung to my thoughts. There was an undeniable depth to his words that made me feel understood. Perhaps I wasn't the individual he was seeking, but his dedication to environmental causes resonated deeply within me.

The dense woods surrounded me, and I knew I had to keep my focus on finding my way out. As much as I wanted to dwell on Pan's cause, I couldn't afford to be distracted. My priority was reaching the safety of the cabin. Only then could I contemplate how to make a difference? Suddenly, a prickling sensation at the back of my neck jolted me. I spun around, but there was no one in sight. A feeling of being watched, like a predator stalking its prey, gripped me. I couldn't explain it, but I knew danger was imminent. Pan had warned me that Bob couldn't protect me anymore. I was alone, and something was closing in on me rapidly. Every second felt like the threat was drawing closer. I had to act swiftly to survive. I quickened my pace, every step calculated, every move deliberate. I couldn't afford to make a single mistake. My life depended on staying vigilant and focused.

I trudged wearily through the dense woods, my breath forming misty clouds in the frigid air. The dim glow of the cabin lights beckoned to me like a distant beacon of hope, promising warmth and safety. A surge of relief and anticipation washed over me as I quickened my pace, eager to escape the eerie solitude of the forest. However, my elation was short-lived as I stumbled over an unnoticed tree root, crashing to the ground with a sickening thud. As I lay there, disoriented and in pain, a sense of dread crept over me. Before I could gather my bearings, a powerful force blindsided me, knocking me off balance.

I struggled to break free, but the creature was too powerful. It started clawing at my back and neck, trying to bite through my thick winter jacket. If it weren't for the jacket, I knew that I would have been torn to shreds by the ferocious creature. I was filled with terror and desperation, wondering what kind of monster had attacked me in the middle of the woods.

I screamed and yelled for help, but no one was in sight. Was this the end for me? Had nature finally won? Tears ran down my face, thinking I was going to die here and never see my family again. As I was lying on the ground, a loud bang echoed through the forest, and the pain in my back made it difficult to get up again. I looked back and saw a dead bobcat with a hole in its head. My jacket was ripped apart, but it kept my body safe. I looked forward and saw my Dad. He had a shotgun with smoke coming out of the barrel. He saved me and shot the bobcat in the head. I stood up, ran to him, and hugged him tight, crying into his belly. He put his arms around me and told me I was safe now.

CHAPTER 7
HUNTING IS NOT FOR ME

As I made my way back into the cabin, the crackling warmth of the fireplace enveloped me like a comforting embrace from an old friend. It was a sensation I had longed for and never expected to experience again. The flickering flames performed an elegant dance, casting a soft, mesmerizing glow that illuminated the entire room. Sinking into the plush armchair, I indulged in the luxurious comfort of the velvety cushions, feeling the day's tension melt away. Cradled in my hands, a steaming mug of velvety hot chocolate released a rich, intoxicating aroma that teased my senses. As I took a soothing sip, a wave of tranquility washed over me, gradually calming my frayed nerves. Earlier, amidst the breathtaking beauty of nature, I had been blissfully oblivious to its inherent dangers. The creatures that had greeted me with curiosity and warmth during the day were transformed by the cover of night into elusive, predatory beings. The forest was a realm of hidden perils, and I realized that to ensure my safety, I needed to be more vigilant and less heedless in my future explorations.

I was lounging in the plush armchair, basking in the tranquility of the surroundings, when my father suddenly materialized and took a seat beside me. His furrowed brow and probing gaze betrayed his concern as he inquired about my well-being. I assured him that I was fine, but in need of some time to recuperate. His next question cut through the stillness of the moment - why had I ventured into the woods alone? I could sense the worry in his tone and knew he was genuinely concerned for my safety.

The truth was, I couldn't bring myself to confide in him, or any of his companions, about my encounter with the enigmatic goat man who had revealed himself to be Pan, the ancient Greek deity of nature and the wild. I was certain they would dismiss my account as a mere flight of fancy, and I couldn't bear the thought of them embarking on a foolhardy quest if they were to come face-to-face with Pan themselves. And so, I resolved to keep my meeting with Pan a closely guarded secret.

Yet, my mind kept drifting back to Pan and our profound discussion about my future. I harbored a fervent hope of crossing paths with him once more before our departure so I could impart my decision. The weight of this choice loomed large, and I was determined not to rue it in the days to come. As I reclined in the armchair, a new-found sense of serenity and lucidity enveloped me. It felt as though Pan had unearthed a dormant aspect of my being. With a deep breath, I surrendered to the symphony of nature's melodies and fragrances, silently beseeching Pan to heed my call and grace me with his presence.

As the vibrant hues of the sunset painted the sky, my father stunned me with unexpected news - we were set to embark on a hunting expedition the following day. Despite my fervent objections, my father remained resolute that I join him. Crestfallen, I sought solace in my room, grappling with the burden of disappointment. Gazing out of the window, my eyes met Pan, and in that fleeting moment, I found myself questioning the trajectory of my life. Hunting stood in stark contrast to my core values and beliefs, yet I knew my father would not entertain my dissent.

As I lay in bed, I pondered every conceivable method to avoid the impending hunting trip. I briefly entertained the idea of startling the wildlife with loud noises, but my conscience couldn't bear the thought of sabotaging the expedition for others. Drained and unable to devise a foolproof escape plan, I reluctantly succumbed to sleep, desperately hoping that the next day wouldn't unfold as dauntingly as I had envisioned.

CHAPTER 8
WE HEAR PANIC

The sun had just begun to rise, casting a warm glow over the group as they made final preparations for the day's hunt. Excitement crackled in the air as they discussed their plans to track down the elusive goat man and secure a prized trophy. Despite a rest-less night, I gathered my belongings and readied myself for the adventure ahead. My father gently reminded me that I would only be observing, as I wasn't yet ready to handle a shotgun. Truth be told, I was relieved by this decision, as I had always felt uneasy about using firearms. It was made clear that our destination was the mountain, the most likely location to encounter the goat man. Despite my knowledge that the goat man was actually Pan, the ancient Greek god of nature, I chose to keep this revelation to myself, not wanting to dampen the group's enthusiasm. With our gear loaded into the truck, we set out on our journey toward the mountains, secretly hoping that our expedition would yield no results.

As we journeyed towards our destination, I found myself captivated by the enchanting sight of the snow-cloaked trees rushing past us. The majestic snowy mountain looming in the distance left me speechless. Its beauty was so awe-inspiring, surpassing all my expectations. Prior encounters with winter had never been this remarkable, but encountering Pan seemed to have transformed my perception of nature. Every aspect of my surroundings appeared intensified, allowing me to discern even the minutest details in the foliage of the encompassing trees.

As we drove along the winding road, we eventually pulled over to the side to unload our gear from the truck. My Dad reminded us of the importance of sticking together, especially after the incident from the day before. I could feel everyone's eyes on me, curious about how I would handle the situation. The guilt from the previous day weighed heavily on me as we started our trek up the snow-covered hill. Looking at the majestic mountain, I couldn't help but worry about the impact of our presence on the local wildlife. Reluctantly, I followed my dad's gesture, trying to push aside the burden of guilt that lingered within me.

As we ventured deeper into the thick, tangled forest, we eventually came upon a small clearing that offered a welcome respite. Each member of our group, including myself, my father, Ethan, Ben, Alex, Daniel, and

Oliver, appeared visibly fatigued and relieved to have the chance to rest our weary legs. I swiftly located a sturdy tree stump to perch on while the others settled on a fallen tree nearby. Meanwhile, Daniel and Oliver were preoccupied with inspecting their shotguns and ensuring they were fully prepared for the impending hunt.

As we settled in, Daniel suddenly posed an intriguing question, "Hey, when we finally encounter the goat man, who gets first dibs?" Ben promptly replied, "Well, whoever spots it first, naturally." Ethan added, "But what if we all catch sight of the goat man simultaneously?" My father, seemingly possessing the final authority, responded, "Then it's every man for himself."

The atmosphere grew tense as I observed their reactions. Before I could interject, Oliver proclaimed, "Regardless of who captures him, we will all share the glory of discovering the enigmatic goat man. We will all become legends in the pursuit." The others erupted in cheers, but I couldn't shake the feeling that their motives were driven by the desire for recognition, while Lucas's pursuit was simply to provide for his family. Lost in contemplation, I grappled with the sense of betrayal towards Pan for remaining silent. However, I realized that I was powerless to alter the course set by my father and friends in their relentless pursuit of fame.

After a much-needed break, my father suggested that we continue our journey up the mountain. We all rose and resumed walking. As we made our way, Ben suddenly halted and pointed to the ground, revealing fresh deer tracks in the snow. Excited at the prospect of finally catching some game, we followed Ben as he led us in the direction of the tracks. However, as snow began to fall heavily, the tracks faded away, leaving us disheartened.

Despite walking for hours, we couldn't find any more tracks or signs of deer. This puzzled me, as my father and Ben were seasoned hunters who should have spotted something by now. This realization left me feeling uneasy and anxious, wondering if something or someone was intentionally preventing us from finding any game.

As we trudged on through the vast expanse of snowy wilderness, a palpable sense of frustration hung heavy in the air. Ethan shattered the silence with a question that seemed to weigh on everyone's mind, "How long have we been walking?" Daniel's response, "About six hours," did little to lift the spirits. Alex added, "Where are the animals? We haven't seen anything all day," voicing the shared disappointment. Ben's agreement with "Yeah, this is weird. What's going on?" only served to underline our mounting concern.

My father, leading the expedition, observed the growing despondency and proposed we turn back before daylight waned. However, Oliver, who had been uncharacteristically silent until now, vehemently objected, "There's no way I'm heading back empty-handed. I didn't put in all this effort for nothing. We have to press on."

As we trudged forward, the slim hope of spotting any game began to fade. Suddenly, a faint sound of movement in the snow behind us caught everyone's attention. Turning in unison, our eyes widened in astonishment as we beheld a young deer mere feet away. Its presence raised the question of where its mother might be, casting a poignant shadow over the wintry landscape.

"Finally, we found something," Oliver exclaimed, pointing his shotgun at the deer. However, I knew it was way too young to be hunted, so I said, "You can't shoot that deer; it's way too young." Oliver paid me no attention and continued to aim at the animal. I looked at my dad and could tell he didn't like it either.

"Hey, what are you doing? This is not right, and you all know it! Let's just go home and come back tomorrow!" I said. Oliver didn't seem to appreciate my intervention and looked at me with an angry look on his face. He retorted,

"Look here, boy, we have been walking for hours, and this is the only animal we have seen all day. I don't care how young it is; I'm getting something out of this trip. Noah, tell your boy to stay out of my way if he knows what's good for him."

I couldn't let this happen. It was evident that Oliver was not going to budge, and the poor deer was in grave danger. Something came over me, and I knew I had to act fast. Without a second thought, I pushed his arms up, and his shot missed the deer completely, causing it to run away to safety. I was happy to see the baby deer get away, but now I was in danger.

Oliver approached me with an angry look on his face, and I couldn't help but step back as he got closer. "Look at what you have done, boy. You made me miss," he said, his voice seething with anger. I knew I had messed up, but I didn't know it would lead to this. "You just made the biggest mistake of your life messing with my game," Oliver continued, his eyes fixed on me. My Dad quickly stepped in between us, trying to diffuse the situation. "What do you think you're doing, Oliver? That's still my son, and you're not going to talk to him like that," he said, his tone firm and authoritative.

Oliver appeared indifferent to the tension in the air. "Noah, you failed to educate your son on the consequences of interfering with a man's hunt, and now I'll have to do it for you," he declared, his unwavering gaze fixed on me. Despite the threat, my dad stood his ground. "You must be light-headed from the mountain air if you think I'll stand by and let you near my son," he remarked, his voice steady but resolute. The others around us stood ready, poised to intervene if necessary.

As I stood there, my thoughts whirled with uncertainty. While I knew I had stood up for my beliefs, I hadn't anticipated the potential consequences, especially my dad getting involved in a confrontation. I felt a wave of helplessness and fear wash over me, unsure of what to do next. In a moment of desperation, I silently beseeched Pan, the god of the wild, hoping for a sign that my plea for help had been heard.

Up on the hill, a dark figure emerged, standing motionless against the horizon. Its form was clearly visible, but it was the piercing yellow eyes with goat-like pupils that held us captivated. We stood frozen, unsure of what to do next, until Oliver reached for his shotgun, prompting the rest of us to take a step back.

In an instant, a bone-chilling scream pierced the air, sending shivers down my spine. It was a sound unlike anything I had ever experienced, a high-pitched wail that seemed to scrape against the very fabric of my being. Instinctively, I clutched my hands to my ears, but the piercing noise cut through me, filling me with a sense of overwhelming dread. As I glanced around, I realized that everyone else had fled, leaving me alone in the eerie silence of the woods. Overwhelmed with a profound sense of helplessness, I sank to my knees, feeling the weight of isolation bearing down on me. As suddenly as it had begun, the sound ceased, and I looked up to find Pan standing before me.

"Pan, you're here; what was that noise just now?" I asked, my voice trembling slightly. "Oh, that was panic, a scream that I let out that sends fear to your very soul. Back in the old days, I would use that to send the army away in fear," Pan replied nonchalantly. I was thankful for his presence, and I couldn't help but express my gratitude. "Pan, thank you for helping. I didn't know what to do," I said, still feeling a bit shaken. Pan gazed at me and offered a reassuring smile, "But you did know what to do; you saved that baby deer, and that took a lot of courage." His words filled me with a sense of pride and confidence that I hadn't experienced before.

I stood there, resolute and determined. "Pan, I have made my decision; I am ready to dedicate myself to the preservation of the wild and the protection of nature," I declared. Pan placed his hands on my shoulders, and a feeling of reassurance washed over me. "If you are certain, then affirm it with me. I pledge to champion the cause of the wild and safeguard nature and all its wonders in the name of Pan," he instructed. I echoed his words, and suddenly, a gentle whirlwind of balmy air encircled me, infusing me with a profound sense of purpose.

"I am proud of you, Joey, for taking up my cause. I know you will do great, and now the wild will always be with you," Pan said, his eyes gleaming with pride. I felt a profound sense of connection with him, and I knew that his wisdom and strength would always serve as my guiding light.

"Pan, when will I see you again, or how do I get in touch with you if I need advice?" I asked, feeling a twinge of apprehension. "You just ask for me, and I will appear. Now that you have taken up the cause, I will always be a part of you," Pan said, his voice exuding reassurance. As I looked around, I felt a surge of confidence. It was as if I had finally discovered my true identity and realized that I had a purpose to fulfill. With Pan by my side, I felt that nothing was insurmountable and that I could accomplish anything I set my mind to.

"Joey, where are you? Joey, can you hear me?" Those were the urgent words of my father, calling out for me. I had fallen behind during our trek, and it seemed he had come back to find me. I turned to Pan, my loyal companion, and promised him that I wouldn't let anyone down. He gave me an encouraging smile and urged me to go to my father, who must have been growing increasingly worried. As I made my way toward my father's voice, I stole one last glance at Pan, only to find that he had inexplicably vanished. Despite his sudden disappearance, I felt a sense of reassurance, knowing that he was still by my side, even if he was no longer visible. Finally reuniting with my father, I was enveloped in a tight embrace. He informed me that our expedition was coming to an abrupt end, and we were making our way back down the mountain. It seemed that my momentary disappearance had caused enough concern to cut our adventure short.

CHAPTER 9

I HAVE A PROMISE TO KEEP

The next morning, I rose at the crack of dawn and began the task of packing up my belongings and getting ready for the journey back home. My mind kept drifting back to the events of the previous day in the woods, but every time I tried to broach the subject, my Dad and his companions quickly changed the topic. It seemed as if they were deliberately avoiding discussing or acknowledging the strange occurrence. Later that morning, Oliver approached me and offered a heartfelt apology for his behavior the day before. He admitted that his actions were rash and assured me that he hadn't meant to direct his frustration at me. I accepted his apology graciously, hoping that their future outings would be more successful.

As I descended the stairs, I noticed that the cabin was eerily quiet. It seemed that everyone had already departed, leaving only my Dad and me behind. As I made my way towards the bar, I saw my Dad engaged in conversation with a tall, rugged-looking man. It took me a moment to recognize him as Lucas, the owner of the cabin. I couldn't help but be curious about their discussion, but I didn't want to intrude, so I quietly approached them.

"Hey, Joey, I noticed you've packed your bags," my Dad said, turning to me. "I've spoken to Lucas, and we've decided to leave a bit earlier than planned." He then gestured towards Lucas and introduced us. "This is Lucas, the owner of this place. Lucas, meet my son Joey."

"Hello, Joey. It's a pleasure to meet you. It's a shame you guys are leaving so soon," Lucas said with a warm smile. I couldn't help but feel a pang of guilt, knowing that he hadn't mentioned our previous encounter or his role in guiding me to meet Pan.

"Nice to meet you, Lucas. Your cabin is amazing," I replied, trying to keep my tone light and friendly.

As my father departed from the cabin, a sense of unease settled over me. I turned to Lucas, the person I had recently connected with, and questioned why he hadn't disclosed his involvement with Pan or his support for Pan's cause. With a thoughtful expression, Lucas leaned back on his bar stool and revealed that he needed to ascertain the authenticity of my intentions. He explained that he had left it to Pan to determine whether I was truly attuned to nature or not. According to Lucas, he could only guide someone in the right direction, but it was ultimately up to Pan to judge one's worthiness.

I pondered over his words for a moment, carefully considering what he had just revealed. I then asked him to elaborate on what would have transpired if Pan had not considered me worthy. Lucas met my gaze and replied, "You would have simply found yourself back here at the cabin. I mentioned that the path has the ability to discern your essence and guide you to a special place or lead you back here." Before I departed for home, I had one final inquiry for Lucas. "How old were you when you embraced this cause?" Lucas paused thoughtfully, running his hand over his chin before responding, "I was a little older than you are now. I became lost in the woods during a hunting trip with my father, and that's when I encountered Pan. He enlightened me on how I could contribute to preserving the environment and safeguarding the wilderness. From that day onward, I made a personal commitment to fulfill that promise." Lucas appeared visibly more at ease as if a weight had been lifted from his shoulders. It all began to make sense now, as we were able to openly discuss Pan.

"Lucas, I'm sorry to bother you again, but I have one more question," I inquired. "What do you do to help protect the wild?" Lucas paused for a moment and then replied, "Well, I'm not just a cool cabin owner; I'm actually a dedicated park ranger. I travel all over Washington, visiting various parks to safeguard wildlife from potential harm caused by people." His words filled me with a newfound admiration for Lucas, and I felt a strong connection with him, knowing that we both shared a deep passion for preserving nature.

"Joey, I have one question for you: what are you going to do to help our cause?" Lucas asked. I turned and looked at the crackling fireplace, the warm glow casting dancing shadows across the room as I pondered my response. "I thought about that, and after talking with Pan and hearing about all the amazing people who also took on the cause, I made up my mind. I'm going to pursue a career in wildlife conservation. After saving that deer yesterday, I feel like I can save more in that line of work," I said, the words carrying the weight of my newfound determination. Lucas's face lit up with a big smile, his eyes reflecting his genuine approval. A sense of relief washed over me as I realized that I had found a kindred spirit, someone who shared the same values and passion for nature as me. Together, we were both committed to preserving the beauty of nature.

My Dad abruptly interrupted our conversation by calling out my name. Startled, we both turned to look at him as he gestured toward the old pickup truck waiting outside. The impatient honk of a car horn echoed through the house, signaling that it was time for us to leave. Lucas turned to me with a wistful smile and said, "Looks like your ride's here. I guess I'll see you around, Joey. But before you go, let me ask you something. Are you going to be able to handle all of this responsibility?"

I flashed a confident smile at Lucas, feeling determined and ready to take on the world. As I turned back to the crackling fireplace, I took in one last look at the dancing flames, feeling a wave of nostalgia wash over me. With each step towards the door, I paused, hesitating for a moment as I turned back to face Lucas.

"Of course I can," I replied with conviction. "I have a promise to keep."

About the Author

Atticus Blackwood is a talented author hailing from Athens, GA, whose literary works seamlessly blend the genres of realistic fiction, mystery, and supernatural elements, creating a captivating and unique reading experience. His stories transport both young adult and adult readers to immersive worlds that skillfully merge the ordinary with the extraordinary, weaving together suspense and intrigue. Atticus is known for his writing style, which effortlessly combines a casual and approachable tone with expert storytelling prowess, allowing readers to deeply connect with his well-crafted characters and enthralling narratives. Fueled by a deep-seated passion for creating compelling adventures, Atticus has the remarkable ability to transform everyday moments into extraordinary tales that continue to resonate with readers long after they've finished reading.

9 798991 423571